W9-AUP-337

Jed and the
Space Bandits

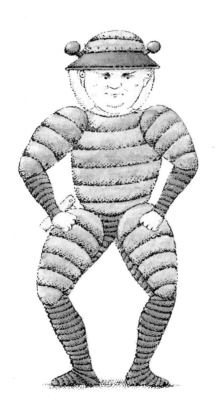

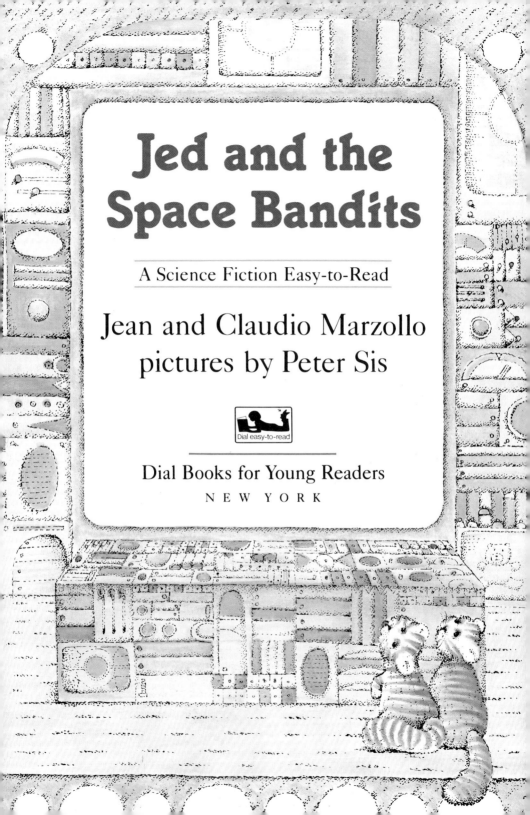

Jed and the
Space Bandits

A Science Fiction Easy-to-Read

Jean and Claudio Marzollo
pictures by Peter Sis

Dial Books for Young Readers
NEW YORK

Published by Dial Books for Young Readers
2 Park Avenue
New York, New York 10016

Published simultaneously in Canada by
Fitzhenry & Whiteside Limited, Toronto

Text copyright © 1987 by Jean and Claudio Marzollo
Pictures copyright © 1987 by Peter Sis
All rights reserved.
Printed in Hong Kong by South China Printing Co.
The Dial Easy-to-Read logo is a trademark of
Dial Books for Young Readers
A Division of E. P. Dutton ® TM 1,162,718

Library of Congress Cataloging-in-Publication Data
Marzollo, Jean. Jed and the space bandits.
Summary: Jed's Junior Space Patrol helps Molly, a girl
who can turn invisible, to rescue her parents from bandits.
1. Children's stories, American.
[1. Science fiction.]
I. Marzollo, Claudio. II. Sis, Peter, ill. III. Title.
PZ7.M3688Jd 1987 [E] 84-15616
ISBN 0-8037-0135-7
ISBN 0-8037-0136-5 (lib. bdg.)

First Edition
C O B E
2 4 6 8 10 9 7 5 3 1

The full-color artwork consists of black line-drawings
and full-color washes. The black-line is prepared and
photographed separately for greater sharpness and contrast.
The full-color washes are prepared with colored pencils.
They are then color-separated and reproduced as
red, yellow, blue, and black halftones.

Reading Level 2.3

*To Ned, Casey, Michael, and
of course, Molly*   J. M. and C. M.

For Lukas   P.S.

CONTENTS

SPACESHIP COMING!

Jed and his Junior Space Patrol were

watching 3-D video on Spaceship Ace.

In his patrol were two cogs

and a teddy bear robot.

Suddenly the cogs started shaking.

"What's the matter?" asked Jed.

Before they could answer,

a voice came over the intercom.

"Jed!" called his mother.

"Come to the control room! Hurry!

Bring Teddy and the cogs!"

Jed put the cogs inside Teddy's chest

and ran to the control room.

Teddy skated after him

on his roller skate wheels.

Jed's parents were at the radar desk.

"There's a strange spaceship coming,"

said his dad.

"It won't talk to us.

We're going to lower the guns."

"No!" yelled the cogs in Jed's mind.

"No!" said Jed aloud.

He took the cogs from Teddy.

"They're upset," said Jed.

The cogs were his special pets.

They were called cogs because

they were part cat and part dog.

They could sense things from far away

and send thought waves to Jed.

"What do the cogs say?"

asked Jed's mom.

"They say someone on the spaceship

needs help," said Jed.

Everyone looked out the viewport.

The spaceship was coming very fast.

"We're going to crash!" yelled Jed.

Quickly his dad turned the ship
and pushed the NET button.

Out of the side of Spaceship Ace
came a giant magnetic net.
It caught the spaceship and held it.
Then the net drew the ship in slowly.

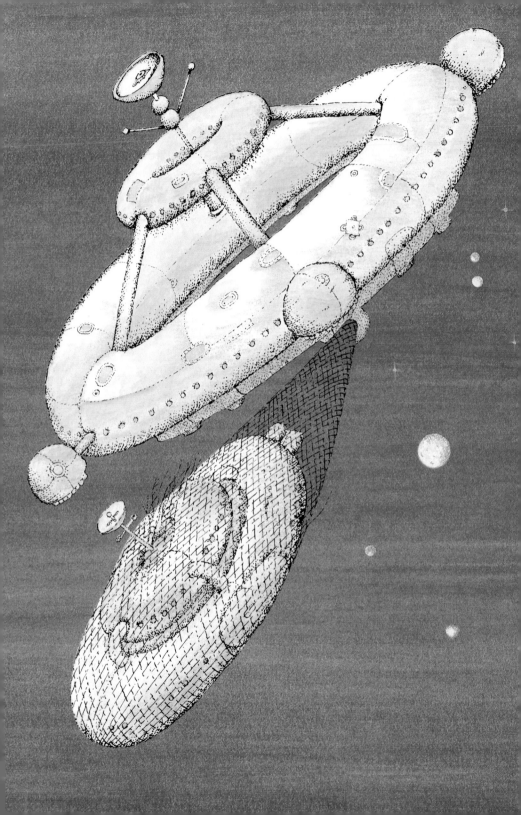

"Mom and I will board first,"
said Jed's dad.

"But WE'RE the Space Patrol," cried Jed.

"And WE'RE your parents,"
said his mom.

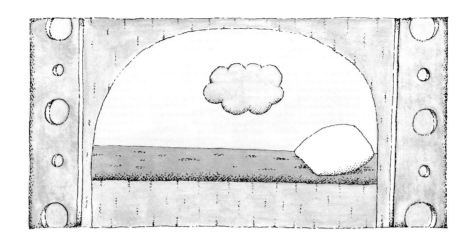

Over the mattress the air turned
into a white cloud.

Then it turned into a pink cloud,
and then into a girl.

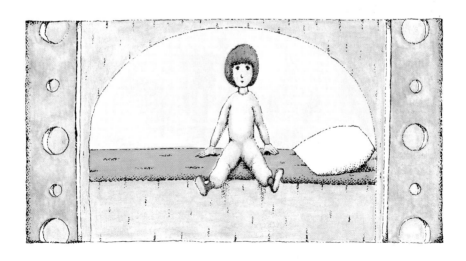

"How did you do that?" asked Jed.

"I drank a new formula," she said.

"Now I can turn invisible
whenever I want.

But it didn't work on my parents.

The bandits saw them
and took them away."

The girl burst into tears.

"Please don't cry," said Jed.

"I promise I will help you."

THE SECRET FORMULA

Back on Spaceship Ace

the girl said her name was Molly.

She told Jed what had happened.

"My parents are scientists.

They made a formula

to turn people invisible.

It's for Commander May."

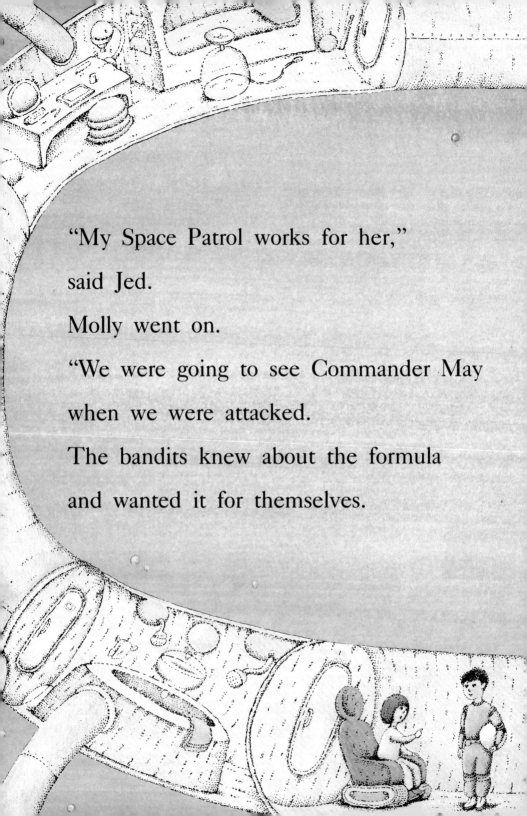

"My Space Patrol works for her,"

said Jed.

Molly went on.

"We were going to see Commander May

when we were attacked.

The bandits knew about the formula

and wanted it for themselves.

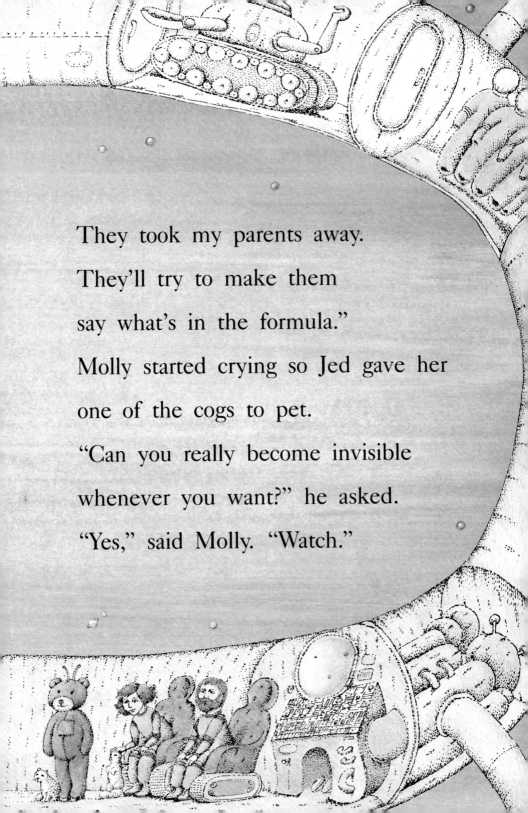

They took my parents away.
They'll try to make them
say what's in the formula."
Molly started crying so Jed gave her
one of the cogs to pet.
"Can you really become invisible
whenever you want?" he asked.
"Yes," said Molly. "Watch."

Molly turned into a pink cloud.

Then she turned into a white cloud
and then nothing.

She still held the cog.

"That's great!" said Jed.

"But why didn't the formula
work on your parents?"

"I don't know," said Molly,

turning back into a girl.

"Maybe there wasn't enough.

Maybe they were too big."

Molly burst into tears again.

"How will you find my parents?"

she cried.

Jed gave her the other cog

and asked, "Do you have any clues?"

"I remember one thing," Molly said.

"The bandits said they hoped

my parents liked frain.

Do you know what frain is?"

Teddy's computer started whirring.

DIT-DIT-DING!

A paper came out of his nose.

It said, "Frain is foggy rain.

Find it on Planet X32."

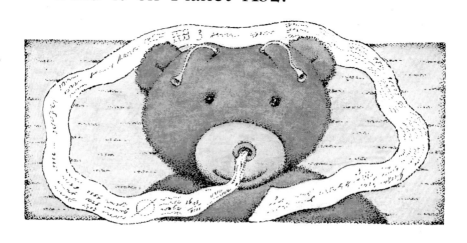

PLANET X32

Spaceship Ace flew to Planet X32.

It was a cold, damp little planet.

The spaceport office was rundown,

and the check-in line was long.

Suddenly Molly ran off.

"Where are you going?" yelled Jed.

"Come back!" yelled his father.

Jed hated to disobey,

but he had to go after Molly.

Molly ran out of the spaceport
and jumped into a little zoom taxi.
Jed and Teddy jumped in with her.

Molly yelled to the driver,
"Follow that green taxi. Hurry!"

Then she sat back and said to Jed,
"I saw one of the bandits.
Maybe he'll lead us to my parents."
The green taxi stopped
at an old dock by a misty river.

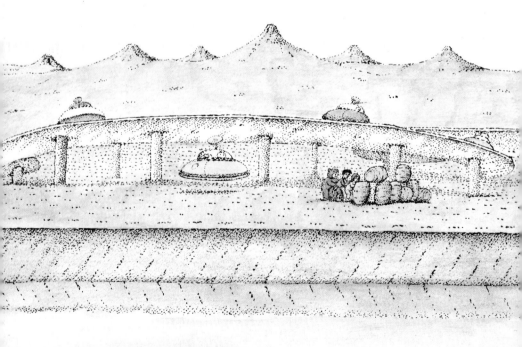

The bandit went aboard
a space houseboat.
Jed, Teddy, and Molly got out
and hid behind some barrels.
"I know my parents are in there,"
said Molly.

"Don't worry about it," said Jed.

"The Junior Space Patrol

has everything under control.

I told the cogs every turn we made.

My parents have called Commander May.

As soon as she arrives, they'll follow us."

But Molly was very nervous.

"I'm going to see

who's on that boat," she said.

"Don't!" said Jed. "It's too dangerous.

Wait until my parents are here."

Suddenly he found himself talking

to a little pink cloud.

The cloud turned white and disappeared.

Jed saw the door

on the houseboat open again.

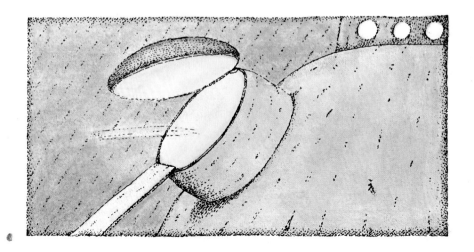

A bandit came out and looked around.

"Who's out here?" he asked,

coming down the ramp.

"Duck, Teddy!" whispered Jed.

But it was too late.

The bandit grabbed Jed and Teddy

by the backs of their necks.

EGG LOCKS

Jed and Teddy were put in egg locks
and thrown into the cabin.
There they saw two more people
in egg locks.

They were Molly's parents!

But Jed didn't see Molly anywhere.

Jed wished his parents would hurry.

The bandits were arguing

about whether to stay or take off.

Suddenly one of the bandits

got his hat knocked off.

"Who did that?" he yelled.

Another bandit's jacket was ripped.

"Cut it out!" he shouted.

Splash!

A third bandit got hit with water.

"I'll kill you!" he yelled,

jumping on the bandit next to him.

In no time

all the bandits were fighting.

Jed was afraid one would fall on him.

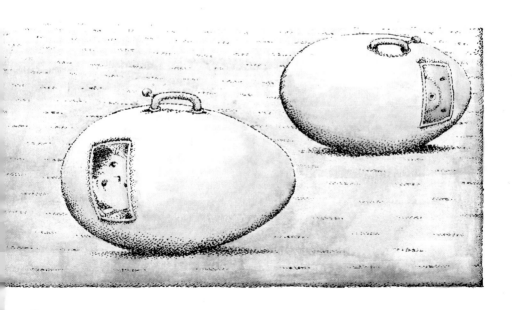

Then he felt his egg

being rolled gently out of the way.

The other eggs were rolled after him.

"Molly?" asked Jed. "Is that you?"

Next to the eggs appeared

a little white cloud.

Then a pink cloud.

Then Molly.

One of the bandits noticed her.

"What's going on?" he asked.

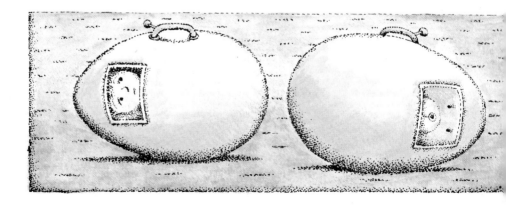

"That's what I'd like to know,"
said Commander May.

She was at the top of the ladder.
Following her were Jed's parents.

Commander May unlocked everyone
and used the locks on the bandits.
Molly hugged her parents,
and they hugged her back.
Then the five grown-ups discussed
everything that had happened.

They talked for a long time.

Molly tapped Jed and said,

"This is boring.

Let's play tag. You're it!"

Jed chased Molly around the boat.

Just when he was about to tag her,

Molly disappeared.

"Not fair!" cried Jed.

Then he had an idea.

He went to see Commander May.

"Can Molly join our patrol?" he asked.

"We could use someone invisible."

Commander May smiled.

"If it's fine with everyone else,

it's fine with me," she said.

Molly's parents said it was okay.

Teddy and the cogs liked the idea too.

"MOLLY!" yelled Jed.

"Do you want to join my space patrol?"

Soon a little white cloud appeared.

It turned pink and then into Molly.

"Yes!" she said.

"Good!" said Jed, tagging her.

"You're it!"